Published by Hachette Partworks Ltd
ISBN: 978-1-906965-28-0
Date of Printing: February 2011
Printed in Singapore by Tien Wah Press

Disney · PIXAR
THE INCREDIBLES

Disney · PIXAR

hachette

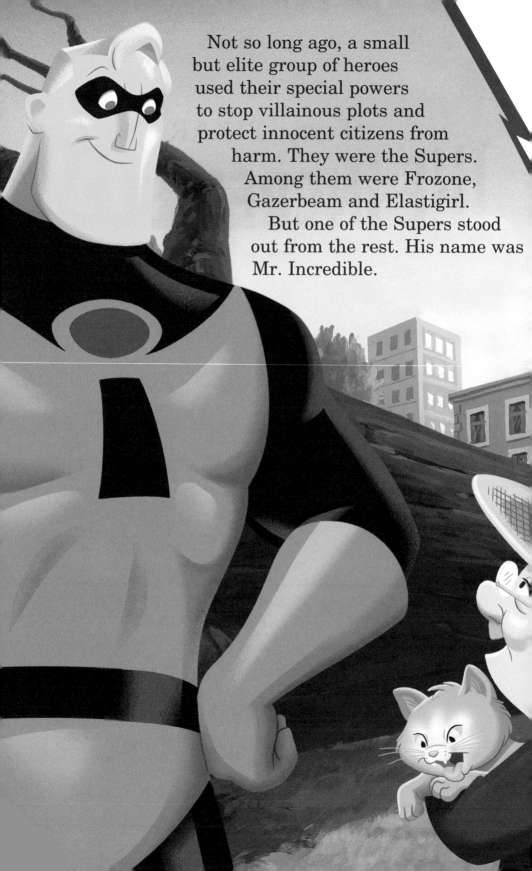

Not so long ago, a small
but elite group of heroes
used their special powers
to stop villainous plots and
protect innocent citizens from
harm. They were the Supers.
Among them were Frozone,
Gazerbeam and Elastigirl.
But one of the Supers stood
out from the rest. His name was
Mr. Incredible.

He was the best-known, most popular hero in the city, and he always insisted on working alone.

One day Buddy, Mr. Incredible's number-one fan, showed up at a bank robbery wearing a pair of rocket boots to help him fly. Mr. Incredible simply said, "Fly home, Buddy, I work alone."

But Buddy didn't listen. Mr. Incredible managed to save Buddy from a bomb, but a bank robber escaped, some train tracks were destroyed and a few people were hurt. It was after that day that the Supers' lives changed forever...

People started to think that Supers did more harm than good. The government decided that Supers should no longer be allowed to use their powers. So Mr. Incredible and his new bride, Elastigirl, became known as Bob and Helen Parr to the rest of the world.

Years passed and the Parrs had three children. They tried to live as an ordinary family. But their two oldest children, Violet and Dash, had Super powers. Only the baby, Jack-Jack, seemed normal.

Like their parents, the kids weren't allowed to use their powers in public. Home was different. Dash used his Super speed to annoy Violet, who would become invisible and fight back with force fields. Their parents had to use their Super powers to break up the fights. Ordinary life was hard for everyone, especially Bob...

Bob missed being a Super. So he and his friend Lucius (the former Frozone) began to fight crime and help people – in secret.

One night as the two friends were rescuing people from a burning building, someone was watching them!

A mysterious woman named Mirage followed Bob and Lucius and then told her boss about them. Mr. Incredible was just the person Mirage and her boss had been looking for.

The next day, Bob was fired from his normal job after a particularly rough day with his boss. When Bob came home, he found a small computer in his briefcase. The screen lit up.

"Hello, Mr. Incredible," Mirage said. "I represent a top-secret division of the government... and we have need of your unique abilities."

She said they needed Bob's help to stop an out-of-control experimental robot. Mirage offered to pay him three times more than he received in his current job.

"The Supers aren't gone, Mr. Incredible. You're still here." Then her message self-destructed.

Bob accepted this secret hero mission. He decided not to tell his family he had been fired... again.

Instead, he told them he was going on a business trip.

Within hours, Mr. Incredible was aboard a fancy jet heading for the island of Nomanisan. He listened carefully as Mirage described the mission. "The Omnidroid 9000 is a top-secret, battle prototype robot," she explained. "We lost control and now it's loose in the jungle, threatening our facility." She warned him that the robot would quickly learn his moves because it was a learning robot. The hero was to defeat the expensive invention without destroying it.

"Shut it down. Do it quickly. Don't destroy it." Mr. Incredible summed it up.

He was finally going to be a real Super again! Of course, it had been a long time since Mr. Incredible had battled an out-of-control robot. It didn't help that he was *not* in Super shape...

WHAM!   **BAM!**

Still, as Mirage and her boss watched on a video screen from their headquarters, Mr. Incredible was eventually able to trick the robot and shut it down.

He even had a new Super suit made by Edna
Mode, former designer for the Supers. When Mirage
called again, Mr. Incredible was ready for another
secret mission. Following her instructions, he flew
back to the island of Nomanisan. Little did he know
he was headed for big trouble!

Once again, he battled an Omnidroid. But this
Omnidroid was much faster and stronger – and
smarter! It anticipated all Mr. Incredible's moves.

The Omnidroid caught Mr. Incredible!

Suddenly, Mr. Incredible heard a crazy laugh! "It's bigger! It's badder! It's finally ready," yelled a wild-haired man who jetted down to face the captured Super.

"Buddy?" asked Mr. Incredible.

"My name is not Buddy! And it's not Incrediboy, either," shrieked the bitter, grown-up Buddy. "All I wanted to do was help you... but I learned an important lesson; you can't count on anyone!"

"Now I have a weapon that only I can
defeat," he added, laughing evilly.
"I'm Syndrome!"
    Syndrome tossed Mr.
Incredible over a cliff,
and he landed in the
river below.

    Then Syndrome threw a bomb
into the water to get rid of the
Super for good.

But Mr. Incredible found safety in an underwater cave. Inside the cave, he discovered the skeleton of his unlucky Super friend Gazerbeam.

Lucky for Mr. Incredible though, the skeleton not only offered a place to hide so as to trick Syndrome's probe, but Gazerbeam had also scratched the word *KRONOS* onto the cave wall before he died.

Mr. Incredible escaped from the cave and then found his way to Syndrome's headquarters and main computer.

When Mr. Incredible typed in *KRONOS*, Syndrome's plan appeared. There was a long list of Supers – and most of them were listed as TERMINATED. It quickly became clear that Syndrome had been killing off Supers by using them to train his Omnidroid. Now that the evil robot was perfected, Syndrome was going to launch it on the city.

Suddenly, Mr. Incredible's suit started beeping.
Mr. Incredible didn't know why, but he did know
it was time to run – from Syndrome's guards.
However, Mr. Incredible never had a chance as a
bunch of sticky globs surrounded and captured him.

The beeping was a homing device that had been sewn into Mr. Incredible's Super suit. Helen had activated it when she met with Edna Mode, who had also made Super suits for the rest of the Parr family.

Helen decided to go and find Bob. Unfortunately, when Helen was on the phone trying to borrow a jet, the kids found their new Super suits. Dash raced around in his speedy suit, and Violet learned that her outfit turned invisible when she did.

"Hey, both of you! Knock it off!" Helen cried.

Soon Elastigirl had everything under control and was aboard a jet on the way to Nomanisan. But as the jet neared the island, Elastigirl discovered Violet and Dash on board. They quickly blamed each other for stowing away.

"You left Jack-Jack alone?" Elastigirl cried.

"Of course not! We got a babysitter! Do you think I'm totally irresponsible?" replied Violet.

Elastigirl phoned the babysitter, but the call was cut short. The jet was under attack!

After watching from headquarters, Mirage announced, "Target was destroyed!"

Mr. Incredible knew that his family was on the jet and was devastated.

Syndrome sneered, "You'll get over it. I seem to recall that you prefer to work alone."

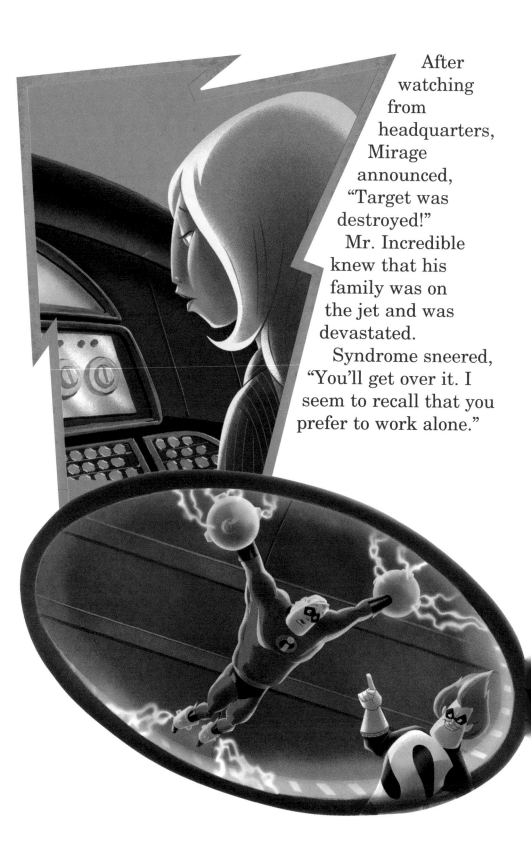

But Syndrome had underestimated Elastigirl. She had made herself into a parachute and landed with the children safely in the ocean. Then Elastigirl had shaped herself into a boat. Using Dash's Super-fast legs as a motor, the Super family raced towards the island to rescue Mr. Incredible!

When they made it to shore, Elastigirl found a cave where Violet and Dash could hide. Elastigirl handed the children masks and said, "Put these on. If anything goes wrong, use your powers." Then Elastigirl left to break into Syndrome's headquarters and rescue her husband.

Soon after, Violet and Dash were forced out of the cave by a giant fireball. It turned out to be a rocket exhaust from Syndrome's base. Dash and Violet watched as the Omnidroid rocketed into the night sky and headed towards the city.

The next morning, Dash spotted what he thought was a talking bird. It was one of Syndrome's security alerts. Suddenly, Violet and Dash were surrounded by guards!

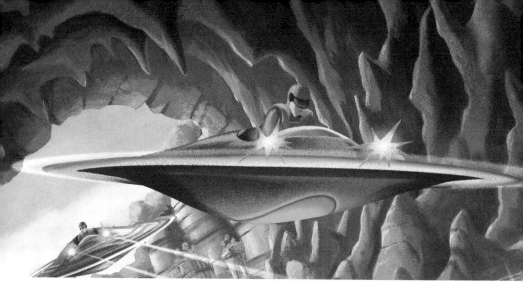

"Remember what Mom said," Violet whispered. "Run!" Violet turned invisible and Dash ran. They used their powers well.

Meanwhile, Elastigirl found Mr. Incredible with Mirage. She gave Mirage a swift punch. Mr. Incredible tried to explain that Mirage had changed sides and was helping him escape, but there was no time...

Mirage announced that guards had been sent after Violet and Dash! Quickly, Mr. Incredible and Elastigirl raced to rescue their children.

KLONK!

Mr. Incredible and Elastigirl reached the jungle. Suddenly a big, round force field rolled through the trees with Violet and Dash inside.

"Mom! Dad!" yelled Violet. Their reunion was cut short as Syndrome's guards surrounded them. Working together, the Incredibles made an incredible team. But they were on Syndrome's turf. Soon the villain caught them in his immobi-ray!

Back at his HQ, Syndrome told the captive family his plans. He had already sent the Omnidroid to the city. "The robot will emerge dramatically, do some damage, and just when all hope is lost, Syndrome will save the day! I'll be a bigger hero than you ever were!" Then Syndrome left to 'save' the city, leaving the Incredibles behind.

Meanwhile, the Omnidroid was already ripping through the city. The people were terrified.

It seemed as if nothing could stop the gigantic robot, but then Syndrome arrived.

"Stand back!" he shouted. He secretly used his remote control and the Omnidroid's arm fell off.

The crowd went wild, cheering for Syndrome. His plan was working. Syndrome looked like a hero!

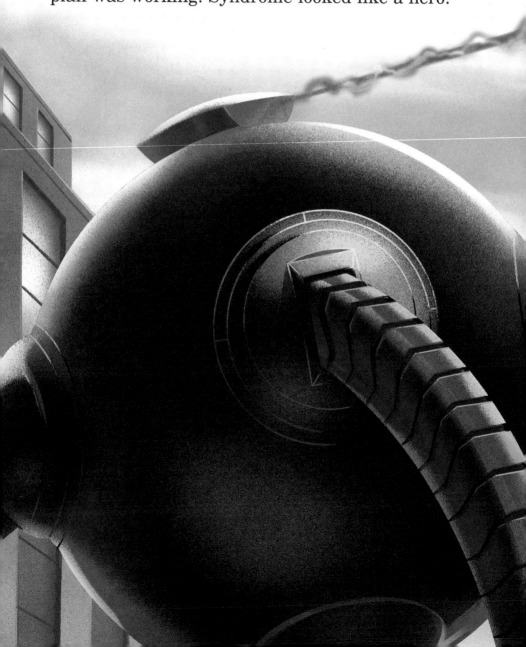

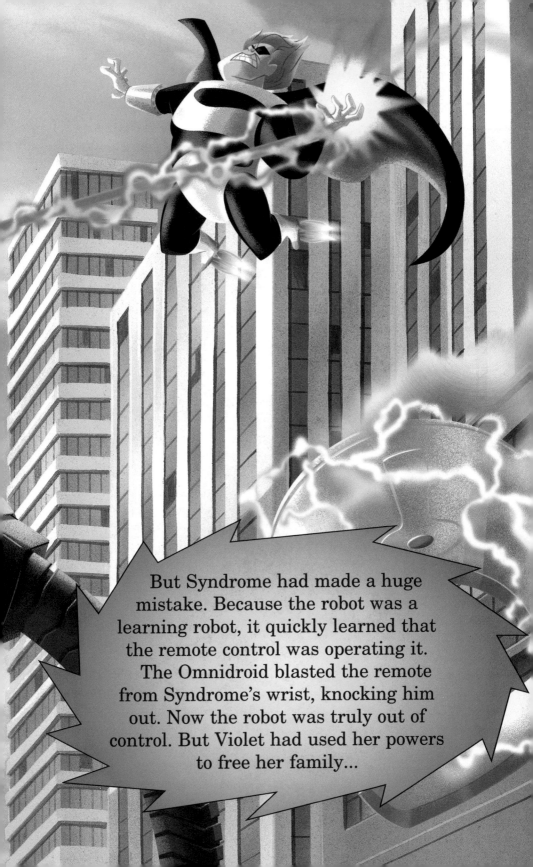

But Syndrome had made a huge
mistake. Because the robot was a
learning robot, it quickly learned that
the remote control was operating it.
The Omnidroid blasted the remote
from Syndrome's wrist, knocking him
out. Now the robot was truly out of
control. But Violet had used her powers
to free her family...

... and now the Incredibles were racing back to the city on one of Syndrome's rockets. When they arrived, Mr. Incredible told his family that he was going after the Omnidroid alone. At first, Elastigirl was upset, but then Bob blurted out, "I can't lose you again! I'm not strong enough."

Surprised and touched by her husband's feelings, Elastigirl replied gently, "If we work together, you won't have to be."

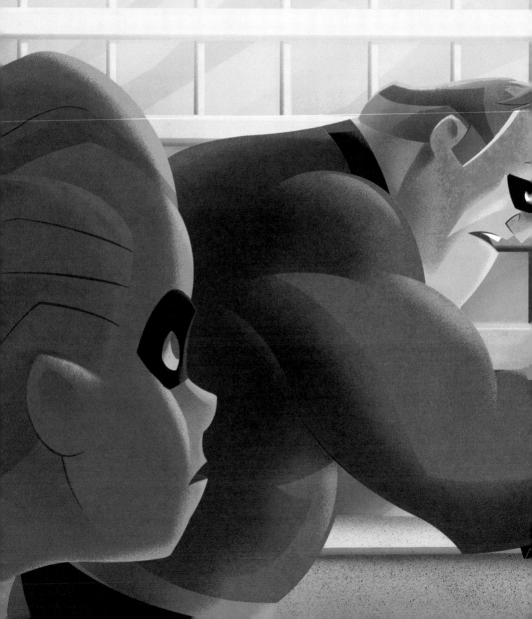

So the Incredible family combined their Super powers once again. With help from their friend Frozone, they were able to trick the Omnidroid!

The Supers had won! They had destroyed the Omnidroid. The crowd cheered.

But the Incredible family's problems weren't over. Syndrome wanted revenge. When the Parrs arrived home, they found Syndrome kidnapping Jack-Jack!

The Incredible family sprang into action, as Syndrome blasted up to his jet.

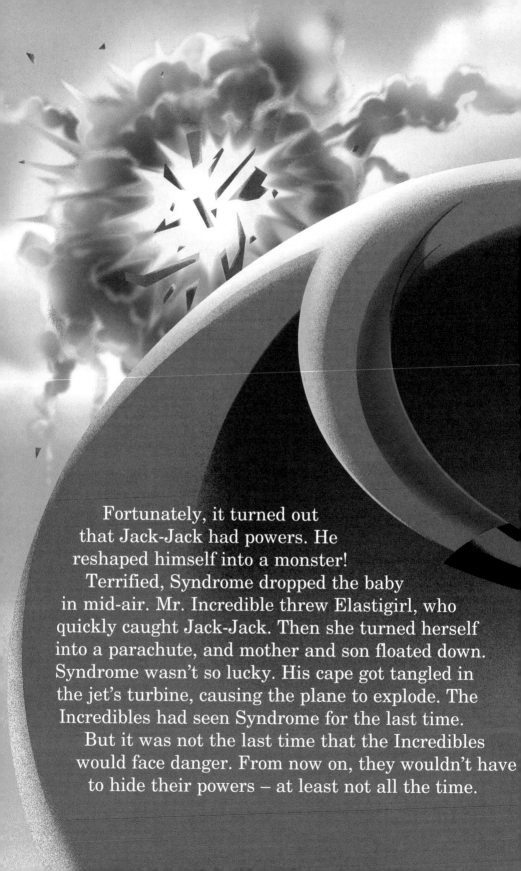

Fortunately, it turned out
that Jack-Jack had powers. He
reshaped himself into a monster!
Terrified, Syndrome dropped the baby
in mid-air. Mr. Incredible threw Elastigirl, who
quickly caught Jack-Jack. Then she turned herself
into a parachute, and mother and son floated down.
Syndrome wasn't so lucky. His cape got tangled in
the jet's turbine, causing the plane to explode. The
Incredibles had seen Syndrome for the last time.
    But it was not the last time that the Incredibles
would face danger. From now on, they wouldn't have
to hide their powers – at least not all the time.

They really were
a Super family!